PARANORMAL ROMANCE#3

Compiled & Edited by

D. Kershaw | Maggie Pawsey | S.N. Graves

Also available and coming soon from Black Hare Press

DARK DRABBLES ANTHOLOGIES

WORLDS	APOCALYPSE
ANGELS	LOVE
MONSTERS	HATE
BEYOND	OCEANS
UNRAVEL	ANCIENTS

BHP WRITERS' GROUP SPECIAL EDITIONS

STORMING AREA 51

EERIE CHRISTMAS

BAD ROMANCE

TWENTY TWENTY

OTHER VOLUMES

DEEP SPACE

WHAT IF?

KEY TO THE KINGDOM

DEEP SEA

BEYOND THE REALM

Twitter: @BlackHarePress

Facebook: BlackHarePress

Website: www.BlackHarePress.com

Cover design	Dawn Burdett	www.dmburdett.com
Formatting	Ben Thomas	www.blackharepress.com
Editing	D. Kershaw	www.blackharepress.com
	Maggie Pawsey	
	S.N. Graves	www.sngraves.com
Read Team	David Green	davidgreenwritercom.wordpress.com
	Jennifer Hatfield	jhatfieldauthor.wixsite.com/website
	Jodi Jensen	jodijensenwrites.wordpress.com
	Lyndsay Ellis-Holloway	authorlyndseyellisholloway.webador.co.uk
	Stacey Jaine McIntosh	www.staceyjainemcintosh.com

TABLE OF CONTENTS

Dandelions
By Stephanie Scissom

The first time I saw Brett, I was nineteen. I'd found a job working security at Dave's Storage Unit. My duties included keeping vagrants and thieves from disturbing the forty rental units that were laid out in five neat rows in the middle of downtown Atlanta and helping customers with lost combinations for their locks. It wasn't the safest part of town to be working night shift, but it seemed to be easy work, and the hours meshed nicely with my class schedule at the community college. I trained two shifts on days and then showed up that Thursday at 10 p.m. for my first shift alone. Or so I thought.

I arrived ten minutes early. A guy in a Fall Out Boy T-shirt sat at one desk playing Solitaire, and a girl with long blond hair had her feet propped on the other, with a ball cap pulled down covering her face.

"Hi," I said, when he looked up. "I'm Jason. New guy."

"I'm Tom," he said, and started shoving stuff into a backpack. "Quiet day so far. Good luck. The crazies come out at night."

The girl lowered her hat and stared at me. She was the kind of beautiful that just stops a guy in his tracks. Big green eyes, full lips, flawless skin... I realised I was staring and mumbled a "Hi," in her direction. Her eyes widened, and she tipped her head in greeting.

Tom looked up at me, eyebrows raised. "Yeah...so, all the keys are in the top drawer of that filing cabinet, along with a master list of the combination locks. Don't give anyone access unless they show two forms of ID and you make a copy of it. They'll fire your ass if you're not a stickler about that. And it has to be the person with their name on the contract, not a girlfriend, not a wifey. Some guy almost got canned because he let a wife in, and she left with his whole stamp collection in the middle of a divorce."

"It was him," the girl said, and pointed at Tom. He ignored her, already heading toward the door.

"See ya, wouldn't wanna be ya," he said. "Night shift sucks."

The girl flipped him a bird, and I laughed. Tom shot me a look I couldn't decipher, but then he gave a half-hearted wave and shut the door behind him.

I looked at the row of monitors and then back at the girl. She hadn't taken her eyes off me, and I felt awkward and flushed under her gaze.

"I'm Jason," I said again, and immediately felt like an idiot.

"Brett," she said, and leaned back in the chair. "Nice to have someone to talk to in this joint."

"What about Tom?" I asked, sitting in the seat he'd vacated.

She shook her head. "He's a tool."

"So…are you second shift or third? I thought I was working alone."

She shrugged. "Wherever they need me."

I guessed they called her in to keep an eye on the new guy, and she didn't want to say she was supposed to babysit me. It was funny, because she seemed standoffish at first, but she was a talker and I loved to listen to her. By four a.m. it felt like I had known her forever, just one of those instant clicks and maybe even more so by the types of conversation people tend to have at those hours. We talked about everything from childhood to politics. I think I was already falling a little in love with her.

She saw me stretch and said, "You want to go outside? We can do a walk around."

A cool breeze blew, but she didn't seem to notice. I couldn't stop sneaking glances at her as we walked. Faded jeans, scuffed boots, black T-shirt and a camo jacket. I probably had close to the same outfit in my closet, but on her, even the ordinary seemed beautiful.

We walked the length of the first row and started down the second when she stopped and touched a bright yellow dandelion sprouting up through a crack in the sidewalk with the toe of her boot. "Those are my favourite flowers."

I laughed. "Those are weeds."

She smiled. "Those aren't weeds. They're wishes. Haven't you ever blown on one and made a wish? And even when they're yellow—that's my favourite colour. They're such happy, hopeful little things."

That made me smile, too. I'd never thought of them in that way. So many girls I knew seemed hung up on materialistic things, and Brett could find beauty in even this small flower. I was captivated.

When we made it to the fourth row, she stopped. Her face pinched into a grim expression as she said, "I don't walk down this row."

"Why?" I asked, taken aback by the look in her eyes.

"Number 27. It gives me the creeps."

It was the third bay door, and it looked exactly like the first two. I didn't understand, but I wanted her to smile again.

"Then we skip this row."

We finished walking the last row. A drink machine stood at the end of it, and I asked her if she wanted one. She shook her head as I fed quarters into the slot.

A payphone I hadn't noticed rang shrilly, making me jump. I laughed at myself and glanced at her. Brett's expression wiped away my smile. She looked terrified.

"Don't answer it!" she shouted. "Don't ever answer it!"

I gaped at her, not understanding. "I don't—I won't—what's wrong?"

She didn't answer. She started walking briskly back toward the office. I chased after her, my change and soft drink forgotten.

"That phone rings every morning at

4:17," she said, as I opened the door for her. "When you answer it sounds like dead air, or there's some sort of hissing noise. It gives me the creeps."

"Probably some automated thing. Wrong number or something, but it's set on an auto-program."

She looked at me and said, "Do you believe in ghosts, Jason?"

"You think a ghost is calling?"

"Don't make fun of me!" she snapped.

"I'm sorry." I held up my hands in a gesture of surrender. "Do I believe in ghosts? Well, I haven't ever seen one,"—she made a scoffing noise—"but I won't rule them out. My grandmother believed in ghosts. She said she had 'the sight' and swore that some people in our family could see them. Some had the gift of precognition, too. She was a very smart, reasonable lady."

Mollified, Brett sat at the desk. "So, do you think everyone becomes a ghost when they die? Or do some move on to someplace else? Why would people be stuck here?"

I shrugged. "Unfinished business? Violent death? I don't know. What do you think?"

She took a moment before responding. "Maybe the unfinished business. Maybe...maybe there just is nothing else."

The easy vibe of our earlier conversation disappeared. She seemed anxious. Stressed. No matter what I tried to talk about, she seemed distracted. When Abe, the old guy on first shift, appeared to relieve us, she walked out the door without saying goodbye. I bid a hasty good morning to him and ran to catch up.

I almost lost her, but I spied her head as she got on the train. It'd been a long time since I had a MARTA pass, so I had to dig for the $2.50 fare. She frowned when I sat next to her in the back, and I realised I probably looked like creepy stalker guy. Too late now, but I didn't want her to be upset with me. I really liked this girl.

"What are you doing?" she asked, and I wanted to run, but the train lurched forward.

"I feel like I upset you and I'm sorry."

She looked at an elderly lady in the next row, who was staring at us. Brett shook her head, like it was okay, but the lady got up and moved toward the front.

"It's not you," Brett said. "But I don't

want to talk about it."

"Let's talk about dandelions then," I said. "They're my new favourite flower. Like you, pretty and magical."

As corny as that was, she laughed, and our conversation slipped back into the same easiness it had before that payphone rang last night. At least, until the next stop.

A lumbering bald man with beady dark eyes got on and took a seat a couple of rows in front of us. I saw Brett stiffen, though he didn't pay much attention to us at all. His gaze fixed on a pretty Latina who sat in the middle, playing on her smartphone.

The rest of the ride, Brett never took her eyes off the man. He wasn't pleasant to look at, but I didn't understand her terror.

"This is my stop," she said, and stood. The dark-hair girl also stood.

"Brett," I said. "Uh, where are we? I need to get back to my motorcycle."

She laughed then; the tension evaporating from her face. "You crazy boy. It will circle back around in about six more stops. I'll see you tonight."

She waved and walked forward, giving the man a wide berth. For a moment, he looked like he was about to get behind them, and I was prepared to do so as well, so she'd feel safe, but he just sat there.

Brett was already there when I arrived that night. She laughed when she saw the small bouquet of dandelions in my hand. Tom's eyebrows shot up. He opened his mouth, then closed it again. He left in record time.

"I don't think that guy likes me," I said.

She waved her hand dismissively as I put the dandelions in water. "He doesn't like anyone. And thank you for the flowers. They're lovely."

So are you, I thought, but I didn't have the courage to say it yet.

I wasn't about to bring up the guy on the train. I hated that tense, scared look she'd worn this morning. But to my surprise, she did.

"That man is evil," she said. "Please don't ask me to explain how I know. I'm afraid he means to hurt that girl and I don't know how to stop him."

My stomach dropped. "Brett...did he hurt you? We need to call the cops."

She hesitated long enough to make me think he had, but she said, "No. I don't know. I can't remember things, and I'm scared to remember things. The phone makes me think of something, but I push it back. Anyway, it's not about me now. It's about that girl." She took a deep breath. "Let's talk about it later. I don't want to think about it right now."

"I looked up dandelions between classes today," I said. "People in the 1800s used to blow on them after they went to seed. If all the seeds blew away, the object of your affection shared your feelings." I shook my head and gave her a pointed look. "You may not know it yet, but I think you're in love with me."

She laughed, long and hard, and I grinned, pleased to see her happy again. Then her face got sad. "I wish I'd met you before, Jason."

"What's wrong with now?" I asked,

with uncharacteristic bravery. "Are you with someone?"

She shook her head. "No, but I'm not what you think I am. There are a lot of bad things, Jason. I don't want to explain, because I really like you."

"You're a beautiful girl with a weird taste in flowers. Think of all the money I'd save on Valentine's Day if you were my girlfriend."

She laughed again. "Just keep talking to me. I hardly talk to anyone anymore, and you're so funny. Tell me about the motorcycle. I'm glad you made it back to it."

"I actually didn't come back to it this morning," I admitted with a laugh. "I got off the train and took an Uber to my place, then hitched a ride to school. Took the train back to work tonight. I was kinda hoping I'd see you." I had seen the creepy guy, but I didn't tell her that. "Come outside and I'll show it to you."

She walked around it, trailing her fingers on the gleaming blue paint. "It's pretty," she said, "but I don't like these things. They'll get you killed."

"I was hoping I could take you on a ride on it sometime."

She gave me a glance that looked like a definite 'no', but said, "We'll see."

Everything was fine until the phone began to ring at 4:17 a.m. I watched her face get that same terrified look and wondered what in the world had happened to her, and if it connected somehow to the creepy guy.

Around time for the day shift guy to

come on, she mentioned the guy on the train again. "I don't know why, but I have the feeling he's going to do something to her, soon. I hate to ask, because I know you need sleep and go to class, but…would you ride the train with me again?"

"Of course," I said.

Abe appeared at six on the dot. "Good morning, Sunshine!" he said, dropping his backpack onto a chair.

"Good morning, Abe," Brett said. To me, she said, "I love that old guy."

I chatted with him for a moment. Brett moved to the door, and I said goodbye to Abe, intent on following her, when he called out, "Hey!"

His old face was pale when I glanced back. He pointed a shaky finger at the Styrofoam cup filled with dandelions.

"Where did these come from?"

The look on his face spooked me. I wasn't sure what was happening.

"I—I picked them for Brett."

The old man's face went slack with shock. "You know Brett? You've seen her?"

"Wha—" I whirled to look at her. She held out her hands in supplication. Tears streamed down her face. For the first time, I noticed she had on the same outfit as she had yesterday.

"I'm sorry, Jason. I didn't—I didn't know what to say."

"Jason?" Abe asked, louder. "I said, have you seen Brett?"

I couldn't tear my gaze from her.

"Apparently, your grandma wasn't the only one who had the gift," she said, and walked through the door. When I say, walked through the door, I mean right through it. A freaking solid metal closed door. I couldn't move, couldn't speak.

Finally, I half-fell into one of the chairs. I heard Abe talking, but it was like he was speaking through a tunnel. It seemed like forever before I could focus on him.

There was nothing I could say that wouldn't sound insane, so I didn't bother to sugarcoat. I said, "You didn't see her, just now, when you came in here?"

He shook his head, his rheumy eyes huge.

I told him about working with her, about some of the things she'd said. Even about the weird ringing phone. When I finished, he just stared at me.

"To be honest, I don't know whether to believe you right now, or to call the cops," he said.

I nodded. It was a fair statement. I don't know what I'd think in his shoes. "She said you used to be a cop, before your wife got sick." I looked up at him. "She said you're the reason she loves dandelions. You told her about how your wife loved them, and how you decorated her hospital room with them before she died. Brett said it was the most romantic thing she'd ever heard."

Abe sat heavily in the chair. "I did tell her that. Can I ask you to describe her for me?"

I did, down to her scuffed boots, and he nodded. Then he reached into a desk drawer and pulled out a picture of her. It was Brett, alright, but on a MISSING poster. The clothing described as the last outfit she was seen wearing was what I'd seen her in.

"She went missing from her shift here, six months ago. I showed up, and this place was wide open. There was a great deal of blood out by that payphone. The police never had any leads."

I gestured at the row of monitors. One showed the drink machine and phone. "What about the cameras?"

"Installed after the fact. Because of her. Too little, too damn late." He leaned forward, giving me a hard stare. "I loved that little girl. She was like a daughter to me. I've brought her dandelions myself. I have never believed in ghosts, but I saw your face this morning. I believe that you saw her, or you're some kind of nut and think you saw her. But I don't know how you know some of the things you know if that were the case. Brett and I worked together some, before we lost personnel and she got bumped to nights. I think she would've mentioned you, and I only told her the dandelion story right before she went missing. You could be the nut who took her, but I don't think so. I can't imagine why she'd share something like that with a person who would hurt her. If you see her again, ask her how much a mail-order bride costs."

"What?" I felt like I'd fallen back down the rabbit hole again. Nothing made sense. I wondered if I was dreaming.

"Just do it," Abe said. "Now go home. You look like shit."

Only when I stumbled to the parking lot, did I remember my promise to ride the train with her. I thought about Brett and the Latina girl. In fact, I skipped class and lay in my bed and thought about them all day.

When I got to work that night, Tom was the only one there. Even though I still felt punch drunk and scared, I had hoped Brett would be sitting there. Abe apparently hadn't told Tom about any of it, because he treated me with the same dismissiveness as always. It was weird to look back and realise he and Brett had never really spoken or interacted at all. I hadn't had a clue.

By 4 a.m. I was getting a little stir crazy, so I jumped up to walk around the storage buildings. I turned the corner of the last one and walked straight through Brett.

I screamed like a little girl. She giggled a little and clamped her hand over her mouth. "I'm sorry. Jason—"

"Are you real?" I demanded. "Am I crazy?"

"I think I'm real," she said. "At least, I was. I know it sounds like I'm lying, but I don't remember much." She nodded at the payphone. "I remember this phone and it ringing. I think he used that to catch me off-guard. I answered it and he hit me with something. I think—" She pinched the bridge of her nose. "I think he's about to kill that girl on the train. Maybe I'm supposed to help her."

Abruptly, she swung her fist at my arm and it passed right through. I yelped.

"Stop doing that!"

Despite everything, she laughed. "I

was just checking. I don't know how I'm supposed to stop him when he can't see me and I can't touch him." She winked. "On the bright side, I bet you look crazy as hell on the security cameras right now."

I scowled at her, then something occurred to me. I glanced at my phone. 4:20 a.m. "Hey, the phone didn't ring."

She shot it a scared look. "What does that mean? Are we on the right track, or are we running out of time?"

I had no answer.

The next morning when Abe came in, he gave me a wary look and said, "Is she here now?"

I nodded and pointed at the chair she was sitting on. "Brett, how much does a mail-order bride cost?"

She laughed. "Tell him I said, 'Ask

Ernie.'"

I told him, and his dark eyes teared up.

"Brett, what happened to you?" he asked.

"She doesn't remember, but we are trying to figure it out," I said.

"Tell him Maggie still visits him. I've seen her around him. She's got a little girl she calls Bumblebee with her."

I told him, and he burst into tears. When he could finally speak, his voice was a gasp. "There's not a soul alive who knows that. Bumblebee was our daughter. She died back in 1974. I've never talked about her since."

"Jason, the train," she said, and I told Abe we had to go.

"Godspeed, son," he said.

When we got on the train, the girl was

already there. The bald man got on the same stop he had previously. His attention was once again fixed on her, but hers was once again fixed on her phone.

I had no weapon, and this guy was twice my size, but when I thought about him hurting Brett or this stranger, I think I could've taken him down with pure adrenaline. We were about to find out, anyway, because this time when she stood, he stood too.

It was still early, not a lot of folks out yet. We followed him, following her, trying to stay ducked out of sight.

She paused outside a storefront and fumbled in her purse for her keys. That was the distraction he was waiting on. He charged her like a bull.

It was terrifying how quickly he seized

her and dragged her into an alleyway. I ran blindly into the alley behind them. He had her pinned against the wall, his meaty hand around her throat.

"Hey!" I screamed. "Hey! Let her go!"

She still had her keys in her hand. While he gaped at me, she swung at his head with a vicious arc. She missed his eye, but the key dug into his cheek. The girl gave it a savage yank, opening up his face.

With a bellow of pure rage, he dropped her and grabbed his ruined cheek. Blood spurted between his fingers, and he ran straight at me. I made a desperate lunge for his legs, but he barrelled past me—straight into the pathway of a Meko's Milk truck.

I'd hear the sound of that impact in my head for the rest of my life. A thudding, cracking, squelching sound. But I was glad.

He'd never hurt another girl again.

Brett was gone. I missed her terribly and hoped every day she'd reappear. I realised that was selfish and then I just hoped she was at peace. There was no grave to visit, so sometimes I'd gather little bouquets of dandelions and place them at the office, or at my apartment. Such happy, hopeful little things…

Four months after the incident with Edward Culpepper (that was his name—I'd followed the story avidly in the papers), I was getting a little overtime, helping Abe go through the stack of delinquent customers.

"Looks like we'll be cleaning out units #27 and #38," he said. "Non-payment of rental fees." He tossed the copies of their agreements on the desk in front of me, and

I froze. Edward Culpepper's face stared up at me from the photocopy of his driver's license. Renter of unit #27.

Abe noticed my face and said, "Jason? Are you okay?"

"That's him," I said. "That's the guy who killed Brett."

I don't know why I didn't think of it before then. Her strange fear of that unit. Now it made sense. I told Abe and that old man moved faster than I did as we grabbed the combination for that lock.

It took us awhile, because the unit was completely filled with old furniture and boxes of junk, but towards the back, we found a metal barrel. On the ground beside it lay Brett's army jacket.

Abe grabbed my arm. "We are not opening that. We are calling the cops right now, do you understand me?"

I let him pull me outside, because I didn't want to see her like that, either.

Brett's body was finally laid to rest. With her mother's permission (and notice to the caretaker so he wouldn't try to kill them), Abe and I did some gardening work on her grave that next spring. Yellow dandelions covered it, looking as beautiful and sunny as the girl they memorialised. I think she would be pleased.

Five or six years passed. I graduated college, got a real job, fell in and out of love a couple of times, but I never really stopped thinking of her. Every time I saw a white dandelion, I picked it and made a wish. When I was in the area, I visited her grave and made sure she still had her cheery little offerings.

LOCKDOWN PNR #3

One day, I was riding my motorcycle up near Nashville, enjoying a sunny summer day. I guess the driver of the Camaro didn't see me when he swerved around a semi to change lanes.

I flew through the air and fell back down, hitting the ground with a bone-jarring thud. I lay there, conscious of sounds and light, but I couldn't move at all. I couldn't feel anything either, except for the heat of the sun on my face.

I was disoriented, but I guessed I was in the median. Lying on grass, for sure, because there was a round, white dandelion inches from my nose. Blackness seeped at the edges of my peripheral vision. I couldn't blow on it, but I made a wish anyway, then passed out.

When I came to, I still couldn't move,

but I felt a little more. Specifically, I felt someone nudging my side. I looked up to see Brett prodding me with the toe of her boot.

"You gonna lie there all day?" she asked and extended her hand.

Surprisingly, my hand rose to grab hers and didn't pass through. She felt solid. Real. I wondered if I was in the hospital and this was some anaesthesia-induced delirium. But the sun felt real enough. I even smelled burned rubber. I let her help me up, and I stood there for a moment, swaying. I saw my bike some yards away, crushed.

"Ugh," I said. "Maybe I shouldn't move too much before the paramedics get here."

She winced. "Yeah, about that…" She

pointed to the ground beside me.

It was surreal to see my broken body lying there, staring sightlessly up at the sky.

"Oh," I said. "Ouch."

She shook her head. "I told you those things would kill you."

"So...now what?" I asked. "Is there a bright light we walk towards or what?"

"You're so calm. I like that about you." She shrugged. "If there's something we're supposed to be walking toward, I haven't found it yet. Maybe it's just me and you."

"Maybe it's my wish," I said, and she raised an eyebrow.

"I made a wish right before I passed out—-died, whatever."

She scrunched up her nose. "Oh, yeah? Is that why I'm here? What was the wish?"

"Just one I've wished a thousand times now. You're really bad about responding to your ghost messages." I took her hands and made her face me. "Sorry. Still getting the hang of this business."

She waved her hand dismissively. "Such a rookie. But tell me, what was your wish?"

"What I always wish—that I could see you again someday, and do this," I said, and kissed her.

I'm not sure how long we stood like that, kissing and holding each other while sirens screamed and traffic whizzed by on the other side of the median.

Eventually, we started walking. I didn't know where we were going. Didn't care. All I knew was that I was with her.

"So," I said. "Who's Ernie and what's

this about a mail-order bride?"

Before she could tell me, a terrible cramp seized my body and I felt myself being tugged backwards. Brett frowned; her green eyes suddenly sad.

"It's not your time," she said. "Stop fighting it."

I didn't want to let go. I wanted to stay with her.

But the tugging became a vacuum until I had no choice: I went hurtling backwards.

I blinked and saw an ambulance worker standing over me.

"There you are," he said as he popped up the stretcher I was somehow on.

They loaded me into the helicopter. I saw Brett standing over his shoulder. She held a dandelion in her hand.

"It's okay, Jason," she said. "Some

things are worth waiting for."

Then she blew on the dandelion, making a wish.

The Lover's Sacrifice
By Galina Trefil

She touched her fingers to the screen, caressing his online photographs. To him now, she was a perfect stranger. To her, in a different time, when he had been known by a different name, he had once been everything.

Overwhelmed with temptation, her teeth elongated and sharpened, nicking her lower lip. That faint trickle of her own blood reminded her of exactly why she couldn't go near him. He deserved a life free from darkness and the macabre.

She fled from the computer, prowling the city streets. Her beloved would remain safe tonight if another man's throat fed her lust.

The Long Goodbye
By H.R. Hreha

Grace paused, closed her eyes, and gathered herself with a deep breath, and then pushed into the conference room that had been converted to a command centre. The team had already assembled, and smatterings of conversation swirled about the room—last-minute details and preparation, side conversations and inside jokes. The mood was lighter than she expected. That, she thought, was unfortunate. On another day the sparks of hope and purpose they carried would have buoyed her own spirits, helped her see the light that laid beyond the darkness. But on this day, they brought no joy. Only deepened the grief she carried in her heart. Grace straightened, braced herself and, without preamble or finesse, delivered the news.

Her words, sharp and cold, cut through the din. Silence rippled through the group and all eyes fixed on her. Fighting the instinct to turn, she forced herself to watch their faces. The first wave was shock and confusion that gave way to disbelief, moving on to fear and anger, and finally settling into horror. It could have been no more than a handful of moments, but as if their stares had weight, she felt a crushing in her chest, all of eternity compressed into those few, tiny slivers of time.

"What do you mean we can't save them all?" Garrett, a crack in his voice, sputtered, breaking the silence.

"We don't have the power."

"That's not possible. We did the calculations; we did them thousands of times." Garrett, voice strengthening, slammed the table.

"Were we wrong?" Cameron chimed in. "How could we be so wrong?"

"We weren't wrong."

"Garrett's right." Grace fought to keep her voice calm and even, to keep her body from shaking. "We weren't wrong. The problem isn't the calculations; it isn't that we missed the mark on the power requirements. We have more than enough stasis pods and had more than enough power to maintain them indefinitely. The problem is that we no longer have the power. The incident last week caused considerable damage. Charlie and I salvaged everything we could. So, we can move forward; we just can't accommodate as many as planned."

Suddenly there was an explosion of voices, a frantic cacophony.

"How many are we talking about?

"Hold on! Don't talk like this is settled."

"There's got to be a way, some alternative."

"Why don't we…"

"What about…"

Garrett, in a frenzy, pummelled the table, jumped up, his chair flying across the floor and crashing into the wall. "Are you saying that this is all because Mel's husband lost his fucking mind, took a fire axe and went ape shit in the power room?"

Mel, face burning, shaking in the wake of Garret's fury, started to protest when Grace put up her hand. "It doesn't matter."

Garrett moved to speak again, but Grace continued, "It doesn't matter. Really, when you think about it, the only thing surprising is that it didn't happen sooner. And the longer we wait, the more likely it, or something similar, something even worse, will happen. As a species, we possess the intellect to understand that the world is coming to an end, but emotionally we're completely unprepared to deal with it. And what happened last week is proof of that. We can't wait; we can't take the chance."

"Wait a minute," Marilyn interrupted, "You and Charlie said you fixed the damage. I saw all the units powered up when you were done."

Knowing this moment was coming made it no easier. "We lied. We're using the main facility power to temporarily run them. We needed to buy some time."

"And there's nowhere we can get replacements?" Ames chirped optimistically. "One of the manufacturing facilities?"

"The only complete cells that aren't in this building are in orbit, powering the NavTac satellites, six of them. Which is a bit of luck because they'll need the data the sats collected when they come out of stasis."

Ames persisted, "Can we get…"

"To one of those facilities?" Grace finished the thought. "Even if we had the means to get there, which we don't, and the facilities were still there and operational, which, given what is going on out there, doesn't seem too likely, we can't risk breaking the seal. Even while cities fall and burn, the plague is spreading, and it's mutating. It's only a matter of time before whoever is left out there dies. Either from the plague, or from the pointless wars and skirmishes that have sprung up, or from all the toxins that are getting pumped into the atmosphere. All we've got to work with is what we have here. This is it. End of the line."

Marilyn brought the conversation back around. "Buy time for what?"

"To figure out what do to."

"And what exactly did you come up with?" sneered Garrett. Grace wondered if he was going to be another problem that would have to be dealt with.

"Crucible."

"Wait, what? Crucible, as in Project Crucible?" Eddie stammered into the conversation, shock spreading across his face, clear that he'd not expected bits of his old life to come crashing into his present one.

"Yes."

"Project Crucible is top secret, black book. You…"

"Really, Eddie? Pretty sure national

security concerns aren't at the top of the list of concerns right now. Bigger fish to fry and all that," Grace chided, annoyed, bristling at the lack of awareness.

Eddie's cheeks turned to two embers. "Oh, right."

"So, what the hell is it?"

"Project Crucible, among other things, led to the creation of Resolution, the most sophisticated and frighteningly accurate predictive modelling ever created. Unprecedented use of AI. The primary goal was the creation of military battle plans with the highest chance of success combined with the ability to adjust, in real time, to changes on the battlefield. And I'd say that it exceeded all expectations, undefeated, as it were, in real world utilizations.

"And as a result of its design, Resolution contained the ability to take any variety of scenarios, such as, you know, the end of the world, and determine what would be needed to start over, to rebuild civilization. Or based on the available resources, the chances of success.

"We loaded all the data we could mine from every system we had access to or could hack into—police, education, medical, military, whatever—for every person currently in the facility. We loaded all the data about all the current conditions outside. Told it how many total slots were available. Then we programmed a list of constants, staff and family associated with Project Ark. The remainder of the selections were made from the other facility staff and family members and the people we brought in from Harper's Mill. Whoever the program selected to give the overall best chance of success when everyone comes out of stasis. It even determined how long the stasis will need to last."

And with the silence, Grace again felt the weight crushing down on her. It all sounded so harsh, cold and analytical. It was; it had to be. They had one shot at this—just one—and it couldn't be left to chance or reckless emotion.

Shaking off the shock, Garrett finally managed to speak. "Where's the list?"

Grace brought up the screen wall and displayed the list. "Red indicates the constants, green is for the program selections."

As the group scanned the list, she

could sense their relief as they read their names and those of their families. Even though they'd been told they'd be there, there was comfort in seeing it for themselves. Pained bits of emotions cropped up as they realised who, of the people they'd come to know, weren't on the list.

Marley had been standing in the corner, silent in his observations, arms crossed. He always seemed as if he vaguely disapproved of whatever was going on, always above the fray, with little concern for others. It was his way, his armour, a crusty exterior that hid his soft centre. Off-putting to most, which was, truthfully, the goal. He was a minimalist in practically every regard, including speech and emotion, so it startled Grace when he turned toward her, angry, and spat, "Your name is not on this list."

"Correct."

"You're not on this list," he repeated, "but your husband, Chris, is. Why?"

She suspected that he already knew the answer she was about to give. "I ran the sim with no constraints—let the program make all the selections. I wasn't on the list, but Chris still was."

Eddie scoffed. "How can that be?"

"The program makes selections based on the skills best suited for the selected scenario from the available resources. While helping pioneer alternative power cells and stasis chambers for space travel is flashy and all that, and has given us this opportunity, there are more practical considerations."

"What about fertility?" Marilyn offered. "That's certainly a practical consideration. You're young enough to have more children."

Grace shook her head, smiling sadly. "There were complications when Sam was born. I can't have any more children. My utility, especially relative to others, is pretty much nil in this scenario."

"And what did Chris say about it?"

"I haven't told him. And I'm not going to tell him."

More silence. More stares. More crushing.

"Look, I'm okay with it. My husband and son are getting a chance. And whoever is taking my spot means that the odds go up for them and everyone else. We're here because we wanted to make a difference, change the world! Clean energy, shooting people off into space to colonise new planets. Now what we've done isn't just going to change everything—it might just save us."

"Might?"

"There are no guarantees. We're using a power source and stasis technology that are essentially experimental. The world is going to hell out there, which brings with it a certain degree of unpredictability for which even Resolution might not be able to account. There's a whole range of natural occurrences that might arise. And the program can't create resources. It can only predict the best outcome based on the resources available."

Not one to shy from the difficult, Marley asked the question no one else wanted to face, "What's the probability of success based on the original sim, with constraints?"

"Less than thirty."

"And without?" Grace appreciated Marley's matter-of-fact approach. It made her feel, at least slightly, less awful. It was all fine and well, scientific detachment, until your ass and the world's along with it were on the line.

"Over ninety."

"Why are you telling us this?" Ames' usual optimism had evaporated. Normally she found his cheery demeanour annoying at best, rage inducing at worst, but she rather missed it at this moment. "You obviously have a plan to deal with the others. You could have just done it—to any of us, to all of us."

"Yes, we could. But Charlie and I thought it was too big a decision for the two of us to make. And we're all here, with this chance at all, because of everyone in this room. You have a right to a say."

"The plan, what is it?" The fire had gone from Garrett's voice. His shoulders slumped slightly in surrender. Grace found relief in his defeat.

"Everyone goes into stasis like originally planned. Once they're under, I'll add a high concentration of EU4 to the feed. It will be painless. They'll go to sleep and never wake up."

"And what about you?" Grace could hear the guilt in Mel's voice. She carried a burden that wasn't hers, and now her friend was being added to the body count.

"I'll finish shutting down the facility.

Maybe watch over things for a while, make sure everything is running okay. And then I'll do what needs to be done; I'll take care of myself."

"It's not like this is settled."

Marley, pragmatic to the end, interjected, "Isn't it? What exactly would the point be if we didn't do everything possible to ensure the human race survives? You want to complain that isn't fair, go ahead. But when was life ever fair? You want my approval or blessing or vote or whatever, you have it. Use the second list, do what needs to be done. If my choices are between saving my own ass for what will likely be a short, pointless time and giving humanity the best shot at starting over, to rebuild, then I choose to give them that chance."

"You could be on the second list."

"I could, but I'm not. I'm an old man with bad eyesight, heart disease and Type 1 diabetes. I imagine the sim wouldn't find much use for me, selecting the more youthful and useful. Which begs the question, what of the children?"

"With no constraints, all the children are selected," Grace offered, what under the circumstances, constituted the good news.

"Can we see the list?"

Marilyn pushed away from the table, rising shakily to her feet, her face drained of colour. "No. I don't want to see it. You can look if you want, but I don't want— don't *need*—to see it. All I need to know is that my children are on that list. So, you do whatever has to be done. Put me in stasis.

I'll go in believing that I'll see them again. And if I don't wake up, I'll never know."

It was all that needed to be said.

***

Grace was bracing herself when Chris came in. He could always read her, sense what was on her mind even when she'd rather keep it to herself. It was something that she alternately loved and hated. Today she hated it. With all the work going on, all the time spent in the power lab, she'd managed to avoid him for most of the last several days. But she was out of time.

He came in, fussing about Gerald who was helping him secure the last of the stores, took one look at her, and immediately asked, "What's wrong?"

Grace laughed, partly out of nerves, partly out of stress. "Well, honey, It's the end of the world."

His eyes flickered, and he gave a small shake of the head, a small exhale of frustration. "Seriously. What is it?"

"Seriously, it's the end of the world. I don't know, it just…I guess really hit home today. Somehow, I had been holding onto some small fragment of hope, even with everything going on out there. Even with us watching cameras all over the world, watching people die, the streets choked with the dead, the hospitals overrun, the fires tearing through cities, war destroying place after place, more and more places where the camera feeds failed, gone, obliterated. The satellites showing more and more pollution in the atmosphere and fewer and fewer signs of life and civilization. The plague, spreading and mutating. Even with all of that, I just kept thinking that someone was going to come up with an answer, a cure, peace and that there would be something left to salvage—that would be how we started over. And now here we are and it's tomorrow. And today is the day we finally gave up, when we knew that there was no hope, it's over. Everything we've ever known. And tomorrow's the day we've been planning for while hoping it would never come. It's flat out crazy, but even with all that, everything I've seen and know, and all the preparation, I wasn't *actually* prepared."

Chris has moved next to Grace and put his arm around her. "You did everything you could, the whole team did everything they could. Think of everyone you're saving."

He meant it to comfort, but it didn't. Pushing all the thoughts away, she sighed and melted into him, grateful her answer satisfied.

***

Chris didn't remember being born the first time, and if it felt like this, he was glad. Everything was a blur, a swirl of sights and sounds sliding over and past him. He couldn't latch on to anything. His head pounded, his stomach churned, and every part of him was shaking; he was freezing.

He closed his eyes and tried to focus— tried to remember what they'd said before he went in. He thought about his breathing—in and out, in and out, over and over. Slowly, the sounds around him began to sharpen, to take form. He could hear the hum of machinery, the release of a seal, a voice saying that it would be the last of the day, another saying to check on Chris. He realised that was him and opened his eyes.

"Here, drink this." A familiar face had appeared before him, bottle in hand, offering it to him. It wasn't the face he was looking for and he couldn't find the name at first. Marilyn, it finally came to him, her name was Marilyn.

When he'd finally fought his way through the fog in his head and asked for Grace and Sam, Marilyn led him to a small room just off the main bay where they'd slept. They'd passed Sam on the way, still slumbering peacefully in his pod. Marilyn explained that they were waiting to wake the children until they had a chance to organise and get things going. Chris understood the logic, agreed with it, but that did little to quell the desire he had to hold his son.

He'd expected to see Grace, but the door opened to an empty room, a single workstation powered up. Marilyn's eyes were flooded with tears when he'd turned for an answer. He burned hot and cold all at once as Marilyn broke the news and his heart. She handed him a small disc and closed the door softly, leaving him alone.

He sat for the longest time, staring at the disc in his hand, wondering if he was still in stasis, dreaming, cause this sure as hell didn't feel real. Anger gave way to grief and then the grief to anger. He didn't know how long he sat cycling through the emotions, struggling. Finally, he loaded the disc and pressed play.

"Hey, babe." He hit pause and studied her face. He could see the sadness in her eyes and wondered how he'd missed it on that last day. And he could also see her strength. And her acceptance. She was always the one. The one who could, and would, do what was needed. Always. The last of the anger drained from him. She'd given up everything to save him, to save their son. It was impossible to sustain anger in the face of such love. And with that, he started the recording again.

"I know you're probably pretty pissed at me about now. But you have to know that I don't regret this. I'm sorry about a lot of things. Sorry that the world went to shit.

Sorry that we weren't able to save more people. Sorry that we're not going to get to grow old together, that I'm not going to get to see Sam grow up. But I don't regret this, making a decision that is going to give you the best shot at starting over, at not just surviving, but thriving.

"Do me a favour? Don't let Sam hate me. I know when you cool off, you'll understand. You'd have done the same thing. It might not be so easy for him. I made a recording for him. For when he's older, when you think he's ready. Tell him, as often as you can, how much I love him. Help him understand that I'd do anything for him. That I did this for him.

"And I love you. Always have. From the moment I met you. I know you think that's bullshit. I remember how *difficult* I was when we met—and that's putting it nicely." She let out a soft laugh. "It's just, I wasn't sure that I believed in love at all and love at first sight. I thought it was just ridiculous. And then I met you and everything changed. I thought if I was a horror that you'd go away and things could go back to the way they were; I could just crawl back into my bubble and carry on. But you wouldn't give up. I don't know what you were thinking or what you saw, but you just rooted like a damn tree. And then there we were, the two of us taking on the world, facing everything together. That's how we did it, how we got through everything—holding onto each other.

"But now I need you to let go. Because you can't move forward if you're always looking back. And I need you to move forward. Sam's going to need you; they're all going to need you. And I can't think of anyone better to help them get where they need to go. They're going to need that stubborn damn tree to get them through."

Grace paused for a moment. Then said all that was left to say.

"Goodbye, my love."

Two Hearts
By Kelly Matsuura

Asleep beside him, Jessalyn looked childlike; unencumbered by duty to anything but her own dreams and desires. Adel stroked her hair and rubbed a fistful of her silken rope against his other palm. The scent of her floral shampoo, although synthetic, made him smile. Elven women smell of nature: rain, sun, sometimes flowers, but there is no selection to it, no conscious thought to add the fragrance for their mate's enjoyment. Human women love to please their men.

Pleasure in *Alfheim* is stolen; moments of vulnerability to one's senses are taken as a selfish whim and made fun of. Men do not write poems of love, nor paint their woman's image on a card to look at on lonely nights far from home.

Adel had never thought of these things until a few months ago when he came to the human world and met Jessalyn. Something in the way her eyes smiled at him made him wish he could play an instrument or sing in a haunting voice. He had only magic to create images of stunning wonder for her.

But his weakness, his inner darkness,

could shatter the life he was making here. The longer Adel was away from *Alfhiem*, the darker he felt. He imagined himself as having two hearts: one, similar to a human's; it loves, and it expresses that love. It protects its soul mate. But the other heart is black; it has no need for love, it seeks only more magic and power.

Adel tried to push Jessalyn away early on, to set her free, but she clung to the aura they'd formed together from passion, dreams, and intimacy. He took all blame for the bond they'd created, but had no clue how to unravel it. It was foolish to think that she could free herself, yet that is what he wished for every time they met.

Jessalyn was human, but that didn't

mean she knew nothing of magic or that she didn't understand she was bound to Adel.

She had had many lovers, but none had reached inside her with only their will and grabbed hold of her heart. Adel had done this and left traces of his dark magic inside her. Consumed, she was. And as bad as it was becoming, part of her was letting it win. She knew she was strong enough to break away from such power and she knew a witch who could help her, but Jessalyn wanted just a little longer with Adel before she ended it.

Adel lay sleeping on his back beside her. She traced a hand up and down his smooth body, enjoying the ridges of his muscles and warmth of his skin. She moved on top of him and started kissing his chest, hoping to make love again before the sun rose and he had to leave.

"Get off me, woman. Don't you know when enough is enough?" Adel's voice was harsh and scared her.

"Wh…what?"

Hard fingers dug into her flesh.

"I'm the one who should be begging for more. Humans don't have the stamina or skill to please an elf. And they are too selfish. I've let this little *indulgence* go on far too long." He pushed her roughly back to her side of the bed but kept a tight grip on her arm.

"No! Let me go!" Jessalyn knew this wasn't Adel speaking, but the blackness within. She broke free and watched in amazement as Adel rolled over and returned to sleep.

"Adel! Wake up!" She hit him with a pillow, but her lover didn't move.

"Fine then. I'm going to take care of this. Today!" She hurried to get dressed and grabbed her purse and keys. Adel would wake in her apartment and have no clue why she'd abandoned him, but that didn't concern her right at this minute. What scared her was that the darkness was winning. It was taking him over while he was unaware, and it wouldn't be long before it had full control of his functional thoughts and the heart she knew loved her.

Adel woke alone; surprised he had not heard Jessalyn dress and leave the apartment. She hadn't left a note, so he didn't either. He rubbed his hands together, generating a ball of blue electricity. Using this energy, he transported himself back to his own apartment across the city.

She didn't know he could do that; he'd only shown her a very small portion of his abilities. He wanted to keep her safe, so let her believe he only had power to heal and perform innocent magic tricks.

Something was wrong, but he didn't know what. He just had the strange feeling of un-equilibrium, like he'd lost control somehow. But of what exactly? Why had Jessalyn snuck off?

Ah, a location prism might work. He hunted around his bedroom drawers for a crystal. Finding a large sky-blue stone, he set it on the table and once again rubbed his hands to start an energy flow. This time he directed it towards to the crystal and asked:

"Show me where my heart's mate is hidden."

For a second, he saw a simple white house, nothing unique about it. Then it vanished and his magic pushed back at his hands.

"What the hell?" He stepped back and looked at his singed palms. Jessalyn went to a witch's house? Why? The protection spell around the property was quite powerful—it would be uncommon in this city so he could probably find out who had cast it and lived in the house.

Disturbed by Jessalyn's actions, he made some breakfast, showered and dressed, taking time to calm his nerves before going in search of the witch and his woman.

He had warned Jessalyn of his Gemini

nature—a dark heart was not something to toy with or ignore. But perhaps he had scared her unnecessarily, and now she'd gone running to a witch. Whatever Jessalyn's motivation, the witch would be sure to know more about his kind than he had told her, and that could never be good.

He called his friend Troye, a Loki. He would understand.

"I'm coming over. I need you to help me find a witch." He hung up, not letting his friend utter a word against him.

"He is not of this world," Genevieve said, without raising her eyes from the bones in front of her. The witch looked and moved like a young woman, but her voice revealed a wiser, ancient soul.

"Well, he's paranormal. I know that. I've seen him heal and do light magic." Jessalyn was a little worried she'd made a mistake coming to see Genevieve, although she'd been highly recommended by a friend.

"There are many paranormal creatures on this earth. Their family lines have been here for generations and live in harmony with the human race. But your lover, Adel, is different. He must have come through from one of the Fae Realms."

"Fae Realms? What kind of creatures come from there?" Jessalyn was confused now. What did it matter where Adel was from anyway?

"Faeries, of course. But they don't like to enter our world. I believe Adel is elven. If I'm right, he has very strong magic, the kind forbidden in this world now."

"He's an elf? Like in *The Lord of the Rings*? He looks completely human though."

"He is not showing you his real image. He has the ability to create any appearance he wants you to see."

"Oh, God." Jessalyn dropped her head into her hands and lay on the table. She had fallen in love with an elf of all things! He may be beautiful in his true form, or not, but either way he was also keeping a huge secret from her.

"And what about his dark heart? It spoke to me through him and tried to scare me away."

"It will do more than just scare you next time, Jessalyn. An elf's dark heart is his true self and should keep the elves coupling with their own kind and away from outsiders. It concerns me that he is here in our world and hiding amongst us. I have not met an Elf here on earth for thirty years or more. Now I wonder how many are really here secretly?" Genevieve got up and walked around her small kitchen, fetching items for tea.

Jessalyn took the chance to think calmly. She wanted to trust Adel, and he had told her about his dark heart and warned her of the dangers, but he had hidden the whole truth. And what did he really look like? She wished she didn't care, but she couldn't lie. His beauty was important to her, and the face she saw when she closed her eyes was the man she loved.

"Genevieve? Can you give me something to help me see his true image?"

"Yes, of course! I will make you an immunity charm specially to protect you from Elven magic. Let me go out back and see what else I have that you might find of use."

"Thank you." Jessalyn sighed, letting herself calm a little. Genevieve's charms would help her find the truth and she could then decide what to do.

"Ah, my friend. What have you done? Gone and fallen in love with a human?" Troye shook his head and took a long swig of his pint. "I admit the girls here are great for a tumble, but to love? I didn't think it was even possible to love one." The Loki sounded cold, but Adel knew his friend had come close to a real entanglement on several occasions. He would never admit it though.

"It's not that simple, and you know it." Adel scolded good-naturedly. He would probably be saying the same thing if the situation were reversed.

"So this girl of yours went to a witch, you say? Do you know who?"

"No, her house had a protection spell on it. I only had a glimpse of a plain white house."

"Hmm, could be Genevieve. She may not be the only witch in a simple house, but she's likely the only one in the city who can do a spell like that or who would know anything about elves."

"I don't understand why Jess went there. I must have done something that I'm unaware of."

"Like, given her a nightmare? That would scare the bubbles out of a girl."

"Yeah, something like that. It means my dark heart wants her gone and things will only get worse. I was hoping Jess had something to balance the darkness, but I was a fool."

"Cheer up, pal. Your situation isn't exactly normal, but that doesn't mean nothing can be done about it." The Loki pushed his stool back and stood up. "Come on! I know a good witch of my own who may talk to Genevieve for us and find out what she knows."

Adel raised an eyebrow.

"You're on good terms with a witch? One can actually stand you?" He punched Troye's arm for fun.

"Let's just say that this one likes my

particular charm." He grinned, not sharing anything further.

"Alright, let's go. I want to get back to Jessalyn quickly and sort out this mess. Hopefully she's not in a bad state." Adel was worried she would leave him, that the witch had convinced her all elven were bad. But she would at least know that he wasn't meant to be in this world, and that alone could end things between them.

Jessalyn drove back to her apartment, texting Adel on the way. She apologised for taking off early, claiming she'd forgotten an appointment with a client. Then she invited him for dinner that evening. She would make Tom Yum Soup and fish curry, his favourites, and hoped that the good food would distract him from her curiosity. Genevieve had given her the crystal to block the Elven glamour on Adel; she kept it tucked in her jeans pocket and wore a loose cotton sweater with a belt to cover the small lump.

She was prepared for ugly, short, grotesque even. Or a plain, utterly boring appearance. But she hadn't thought he could be even more beautiful than she already saw him. When she opened the door, she could only stand there and stare in a daze.

The pointed ears were there. Expected, but still a surprise. His hair, as black and glossy as a raven's was tied in a high ponytail, with both sides shaved in intricate patterns. His face was similar to the one he usually wore, but slenderer and more defined. Dark green eyes like mirrors glowed despite the dim light in the hallway. He wore no shirt, only loose grey pants and black leather boots. His bare chest was a landscape of ridges and roads, smooth muscle scarred by small knife or possibly arrow wounds. Tattooed symbols trailed down both arms—Jessalyn recognised some as runes. He was, simply, magnificent, and all thought of leaving him vanished.

"Are you okay?" he asked, brushing her cheek with a finger.

His heat rippled right through her body. Oh God! His glamour was protecting me from the true power of his beauty! Jessalyn wanted to hide the crystal as soon as she could—she didn't want to look at him like this any longer. It was too hard to hide her twirling emotions.

"Ah yeah, I'm fine. Sorry about earlier. I should've left a note, but I was really late."

"No problem. Hey, I smell Thai food! Great!" He pushed his way in and moved to the kitchen.

While he poured them both wine, Jessalyn tossed the crystal in the back of the utensils drawer. When she turned back around, she saw the Adel she was used to, just a regular guy in faded jeans and a grey print T-shirt. Still as gorgeous as sin, but not spell-binding beyond belief.

Adel watched Jessalyn throughout dinner. Apart from being a bit jittery, she was her usual bubbly self. If she'd learned something terrible from Genevieve, she was good at hiding her feelings. Troye's witch friend had promised to ask around and find out who Jessalyn had gone to see, but Troye hadn't called Adel back yet about it.

After washing the dishes, he pulled Jessalyn into his arms. Despite the tension of the day, being close to her somehow calmed him, and he wanted to connect with her.

"I love you, desperately," he confessed, needing her to see he meant it.

She gazed up at him while tracing her nails lightly down his bare arms.

"I know you do. And I love you..."

"But?"

"You keep warning me our love is dangerous, but I'm still not sure why. You push me away and then pull me back again. I really can't take much more of it." She spoke so quietly. The witch had given her doubts about his commitment to her.

"If I don't tell you things, about what I am, or where I'm from, it's to keep you safe."

"I'm not afraid of your family or your people. Or anyone else that may want to tear us apart. But I'm scared of the darkness in you. That's where the biggest danger lies. Within *you.*"

He stepped away from her and turned away, needing space.

"I would never hurt you!" he pleaded over his shoulder. He fought to contain the anger inside. Seeing a chance to break them, the darkness was pushing out. He felt it choking him, wanting to take his voice and manipulate it.

"I know you won't Adel, but you can't control the evil in your heart. It wants me gone."

He heard her fumbling in the drawers for something. Did she have a weapon? Was she truly frightened? He spun around.

"What are you doing?!" He grabbed her arm, and she struggled to hide whatever she was holding.

"Just stop!" She broke free and ran to the bedroom, slamming and locking the door.

The dark heart wanted to break it down and fought to make him do so, but with Jessalyn safe and out of sight he found it easier to take back control. He took deep calming breaths and stopped outside the bedroom door.

"Jess, I'm sorry. I don't want to scare you. I can control it, I promise!"

"Why is this happening? Why can't we just be together?" Her voice broke into gasping sobs.

"I'm sorry. And, I'm going to fix it. I just need a bit more time." He waited for an answer, but she stayed silent.

"Jessalyn? Talk to me."

Still silence. He couldn't stand being ignored.

He pushed hard against the door and the lock snapped.

"I'm not going to hurt you. Let's just talk." He looked around the tiny bedroom, but she was not there.

"Jess?" The single window was locked tight. How the hell had she disappeared?

Jessalyn opened her tear-filled eyes and found herself in Genevieve's living room.

"Oh, thank God it worked!"

"Of course it did! Now sit down and I'll make you some brandy tea."

Jessalyn dropped the crystal on the coffee table and noticed her hands were shaking badly. Teleporting via magic was more hair-raising than any rollercoaster she'd even ridden. Still she was grateful for the witch's idea to attach a transport spell to the crystal so that she could escape if she felt in danger.

She had placed the crystal in the drawer, foolishly thinking she didn't need it that evening. But when the dark power started appearing in Adel, she just had to see if he looked any different when he lost control. Sure enough, the crystal had allowed her to see the dark elf's red eyes and wicked thin-lipped mouth. Adel had less control than he believed.

Genevieve joined her with the tea and Jessalyn explained what had happened with Adel.

"Hmm, a troublesome business. I did some research after you left. I believe Adel is a race of elf known as the Gemini's. They're dark elves but not considered evil, just a strong race of warriors in *Alfhiem*, the elf realm. But they are connected to their leader, Queen Alfaire. They are not permitted to leave *Alfheim* because here they lose their connection to her and that's when the darkness takes over."

"Oh, you mean they're like a hive

collective? Are they telepathic?"

"Yes, that's right. In *Alfheim* they are subservient and good-natured due to their fair queen. She is said to be noble and keeps peace in the land."

"Why would Adel leave? Could he have been banished?" Jessalyn couldn't imagine Adel would simply run away from his duty.

"No, I wouldn't imagine so. Perhaps he came here on a mission of some kind, but cannot return safely. I would really like to ask him if we can orchestrate a situation where his darkness is not threatened, and we can discover the truth to all this."

Troye came through with Genevieve's address, but Adel refused his friend's offer to accompany him. He would go alone and beg the witch to help him overcome the darkness. It was something he should have done a month ago, but he had always mistrusted witches and he had let his pride block his senses in this case.

He didn't knock—he found the door was left open. He had no doubt the witch knew he would find them there.

She met him in the hallway and gestured that he enter the living room.

"Hello, Adel. Jessalyn is in here. Come." She smiled warmly but Adel was still wary.

"No funny business, Genevieve. I'm not a threat to either of you; I just want to talk. I need your help."

She laughed.

"Of course you do! Don't worry, Jessalyn and I have been talking, and we think we've found a solution to your problem."

"Really?" Hope soared in him. But was it a trick?

He stepped into the living and was relieved to see Jessalyn sitting on the sofa drinking tea.

"Jess! What the…?" He moved to go to her, but his eyes caught the layer of magic glimmering between them.

"I put a ward up to protect her. Just in case you let loose the darkness."

He sighed. He should argue it wasn't necessary, but perhaps it was.

"Sit down, Adel. And you may as well drop your glamour. We can both see your true form."

"What?" Adel looked at Jessalyn, who had stood up and was smiling.

"Genevieve gave me a crystal to show me past your glamour. You are so amazingly beautiful, Adel. I can't believe you didn't show me your true form before."

"You like me like this? I don't scare you?"

"Only my heart. I'm scared you will enchant me for the rest of my days, whether you love me back or not."

"Love you back…of course... Oh, you're teasing, I see." He smiled. Inside, he was dancing because she accepted what he was. He was a fool, for sure.

"Genevieve, can you help us? I can't live without her, and we both can't continue this nightmare any longer."

Genevieve sat down in her own chair.

"I believe I can help you, but first you must tell us why you are here on Earth and have not returned to *Alfhiem*. Are you in some kind of trouble?"

"No, not exactly. I came with a small party to capture a band of dark elves that had crossed over illegally. We caught them and went to return through the gate, but I couldn't pass through it. Everyone else did except me. I just couldn't walk through it."

"How strange," Jessalyn said. "When was this?"

"The day after we met." He hung his head, remembering how the second he'd seen her in the restaurant that night he had needed her. He had seduced her in minutes and spent the night at her house, but the tables were turned, and he had found himself captivated by this human girl.

He looked at both the women, ready to tell the truth.

"I think I couldn't pass through the gate because I'd fallen in love with a human. I'd made some connection with Jessalyn instantly, and I simply couldn't leave her."

"That's true? Even then?" Jessalyn wiped her eyes and placed a hand to her heart.

"Yes! I didn't know it at the time, but I'm sure now."

"It's about what I thought," Genevieve said, putting her teacup down. "Adel, you are a warrior, loyal to your queen and Elven collective. But you have bonded with Jessalyn in this world and have disengaged with your life and duty in *Alfheim*."

"So, his darkness is Queen Alfaire, pulling him back?" Jessalyn asked.

"No, the opposite actually. In *Alfheim*,

the queen is the anchor for his goodness. She gives him the strength to keep his inner darkness inert. The Gemini Elves are a slave race, harsh to say, but true. Without a leader of good intent, overtime the Gemini would become vicious and filled with hate." Genevieve looked back and forth between them.

"Adel, you have somehow broken free of the tether between you and Queen Alfaire and you have created a new one with Jessalyn, but it has not fully anchored you here yet."

Realisation dawned on Adel. He had known he loved her but had not realised that he had transferred his loyalty to her. He would protect her over his queen in a heartbeat; therefore, he had to admit that Genevieve was right.

"So I must be someone's slave in order to anchor, as you said, myself to goodness."

"What?" Jessalyn looked startled. "You are *not* going to be my slave, Adel. I want to be your partner, but I am no queen. I have no magic to strengthen you."

"You don't need magic, dear. You just need a pure heart that is worthy of his devotion. You need to believe in his strengths: honour, courage, and loyalty. You must guide him through his days and see that he always has a purpose, a reason to serve you."

"I don't need a slave! For God's sake…this is ridiculous!" Jessalyn began pacing in her sequestered space. "I'm no one. I don't need an elf-warrior to protect me when I go to work at the clinic. No offense, Adie." She calmed when she realised her words might hurt his feelings, but he laughed.

"None taken. You are certainly a strong woman and haven't needed my strength or magic for anything so far. Genevieve, I wish it were true. I would gladly serve Jessalyn as my queen, but I must have some purpose here to stay permanently."

"Certainly. You need an anchor. It doesn't have to be a queen with an empire to guard, just something fragile and in need of your protection and teaching as it finds its own way in the world." She sat back, somewhat smugly.

"What do you mean by that?" he asked.

"I think she means…a baby. Right,

Genevieve?" Jessalyn was blushing as she looked to the witch for confirmation.

"Of course that's what I mean! Wasn't I clear enough? When Jessalyn becomes pregnant with your child, your bond will be complete. The darkness will never surpass your love for them both. Your connection to your family will be stronger than any feeling you experienced with your queen or previous masters."

Adel was quite speechless. A child! He had never considered it before. Being one of Queen Alfaire's elite warriors, he had committed himself to his position and had never questioned it. The idea of a child half-elf and half-human filled him with a sudden urge to cry. Elves do not cry! He scolded himself but broke into a grin. "When do we start?"

BLACK HARE PRESS

First published, *Parting Skies*, 2013

A Solitary Dream
By Kimberly Rei

"Hold on," he whispered as the winds swirled and the balloon rose higher. She shivered in his arms, staring in wonder at the boat below. Smaller and smaller, until the people vanished and their only companions were the birds soaring around them.

Two white scarves, one for each of them, were tied to the balloon and flapped in the growing wind. They had scrawled their most secret dreams across the cloth, not caring if the ink smeared or the words were illegible. Dreams, after all, are not for confining in cage or script. They must remain free to become what they will.

He nuzzled her neck, his smile raising a line of goosebumps.

Her hand tightened on his arm, "Will you forgive me? Will you love me forever?"

"Of course," he said. If sadness laced his soft, understanding voice, they didn't acknowledge it. They had spoken long into many nights about this journey.

When the boat was all but a speck and even the birds had given up such mighty heights, she reached out to her dream-silk and pulled it loose. He watched it catch the wind and spin, swirling until it was torn away. He felt her shift in his arms and he held tight as tears streamed down his cheeks. When her beak struck his arm and her wings battered his face, he released her and watched as his dearest love flew off into the blue, blue sky.

He reached for his own silk, leaving it attached. It held one word, his only dream, over and over. Her name.

The Perfect First Date
By Celestine Trinidad

Amaya was dreaming. That had to be the only logical explanation for this. Any moment now she would be waking up in her condo and remember that she was—always has been and maybe always will be—alone. But no, this vision of a man was still standing before her, lips turned up in a smile that seemed to reach all the way up to his eyes, which were a rich, warm brown colour, like his own perfectly tanned skin. *Like warm caramel,* the thought came to her, unbidden. He was taller than she had expected, and she suddenly wished she hadn't worn flats today, for if she stood, she wouldn't even reach up to his shoulders. His black hair was slightly ruffled, and yet it still seemed like he intended for it to look that way. His charcoal grey shirt even fit his form perfectly, accentuating well-toned arms and broad shoulders.

For Bathala's sake, her blind date was hot. No—*very* hot. That had never happened before. Since the Bathala's Gift app was a blind dating site, she never saw what her matches looked like before she actually met them. As the app developers claimed, she did not need to see how they looked like, because Bathala Himself meant for her to meet these guys. Supposedly the app factored in her personal preferences with the Divine Will, since the app's algorithm was made by Babaylan constantly in communion with Bathala Himself. But after an entire year of using the app, she never really met anyone who she was interested in seeing for more than two dates. And well, it was beginning to look like it was Bathala's will to date guys that were just…okay. Or at most, passably cute.

But this guy was more than passably cute. More than just…*okay.*

"Mar—" Her voice came out as a croak, to her utter mortification. She cleared her throat and tried again. "Marco?" She smoothed down the hair she kept in a loose ponytail and adjusted her black dress. Maybe she should have worn red, like her friends kept telling her.

"Yes," he said. "Amaya, right?"

She could only nod. *Bathala help me, even his voice is sexy*—low and husky like that. Did he just wake up or did he always sound like that? She didn't know if she could handle it if it was the latter.

Maybe he was a Diwata? He certainly looked like one. But these days even humans could look as good as the Diwata, what with cosmetic surgery and the plethora of beauty products on the market, so maybe not. In the first place, why in the world would a Diwata be matched to her? She had checked her ancestry before, and she didn't have an ounce of Diwata blood in her at all. Sure, the days when the Diwata were worshipped by humans as deities were long gone, but intermingling between the races was still uncommon. The Diwata would *never* deign to be with a human, that was for sure.

He sat down across from her, and as he did she caught a whiff of his cologne—was that Apolaki Eros? Bantugan Red Intense? Whatever it was, and whatever happened after this, she would now forever associate this scent with him.

"So um, you're early," she said, looking at her watch to avoid looking at him.

"You are, too," Marco said with a grin. "Hey, thanks for accommodating the sudden change of time and venue of our first date. This is nearer to where I'm supposed to meet my client at 1 PM. Really sorry, this happens at work far too often."

Okay. His work. That was a safe topic to start with. Amaya's anxiety was beginning to have her stomach in knots. "Ah, I see. You're a lawyer, right?"

"Yes," he replied. "You know how it is. High-profile client, related to some congressman or the other, demanding that we accommodate her at once, so I suddenly had an appointment at 1."

"No worries, really," she said. "We could even have moved it up to tomorrow. I mean, what's one more day?"

"We don't know what could happen tomorrow."

She looked up at him. His tone was still light, but his eyes suddenly seemed less warm. Distant, unreadable.

"And well, I hate turning down a commitment," he said after that moment of silence. He smiled, and just like that, the warmth was back in his eyes. "Not a good impression to make on a first date, you know. And you're my very first date through the app, if you must know."

"Oh, so this is your first time using the app?"

He nodded. Well, she was right, then. Someone who looked like *him* probably didn't need apps like this one to meet people. But that still left another burning question: "So why did you try it this time?"

"I just wanted to check it out," he said. "It seemed like a better way to meet more people."

Amaya's heart sank. What if he was

one of those Diwata who wanted to try "roughing it", mingling with the commoner humans because they were bored with their perfect lives in their gated villages and towering mansions? He did say in his profile that he was looking for a serious relationship, though. But maybe that was just a ploy?

She shook her head. *Stop it, Amaya.* She did this every time. Her friends told her she always judged her dates a little too much. It came from her line of work, and even though she tried her best not to, it somehow always bled into her personal life. They told her maybe it was why she was single, and why the app wasn't working for her as well as it should. But there were always little clues that gave away someone's personality, and she didn't want to bother giving these men chances she knew they didn't deserve.

"Good morning, ma'am, sir." Their waiter finally arrived, interrupting her musings. "My name is Glen, and I will be your server today." He pointed at the nameplate pinned on his shirt. "Would you be interested in getting some appetisers?"

She and Marco gave their orders, which Glen promptly punched into his tablet. After a second's hesitation, she asked Glen, "Um, are you serving cocktails even at this hour?"

Glen smiled. "Yes, ma'am."

"Okay." She would need something stronger if she was going to make it through this date. "Gin and tonic then, please."

She glanced at Marco, expecting

surprise or disapproval in his expression, but he was grinning. "Make that two, please." Damn, she wished he would stop smiling like that. With his eyes twinkling like that, they were almost mesmerising.

"Is that your favourite drink, then?" he asked.

She shrugged. "Yeah, I guess," she said. "I mean, it's actually bitter, but it's…comforting. It's been a long week."

"Why? Did anything happen?"

She looked up at him and was surprised to see how concerned he really seemed. It even matched the earnestness in his tone. "But I understand if you wouldn't be comfortable telling me," he added.

"Uh," she said. She didn't know why, but she somehow felt like she would be comfortable talking to him about it. "It's about work. Nothing interesting, really."

"Ah, I see," he said. "Your profile didn't say anything about your line of work."

"I'm a writer."

"What kind of writing do you do?" Before she could open her mouth to reply he suddenly blurted out, "Wait. Wait. Are you Amaya Dela Fuente?"

Amaya pursed her lips at that. Oh, no. Her friends kept warning her about this. *Don't, for the love of Bathala, DON'T talk about your work on the first date! You know that would only lead to talking about politics, and you know what happens when you get to talking about THAT.* She made the mistake of doing that on the very first date through the app, and that somehow led her to walking out even before their food arrived.

"I've read your articles and opinion columns," he was going on even as she hesitated. "I even follow you on Twitter. By Bathala, this is amazing."

She stared at him. "You like my articles?"

"Yes," he said. "Your pieces are highly critical, and yet still level-headed and very educational. I particularly liked that last article you made on Duli's time as mayor of the Southern Isle of Digos." His eyes darkened. "All those lives lost in his supposed crusade against crime in his city. And nobody cared because they were Lamang Lupa anyway. Just because everyone thinks they're monsters, they don't deserve mercy, or even at least justice. And it's happening again now, here."

"You…" She swallowed the lump in her throat. "You don't call Duli 'Ama'."

His eyes blazed. "Why would I? He's not *my* father."

"I…" She stood up, suddenly. "I need to go to the washroom. Excuse me."

She fled to the washroom, and when she found an empty stall, she leaned on the door and closed her eyes.

This was impossible. Her date was not only hot, but he was also unsympathetic to the highest Diwata in the land right now—the President of the United Isles of the Archipelago. Amang Duli, they called him. *Our Father Duli.* She had been highly critical of his administration in her articles, and many people were angered by her reports. But people deserved to know the truth. The "peace" that Duli so proudly claimed he brought to Digos, and now, the rest of the archipelago, had claimed the lives of many innocent Lamang Lupa, the third race, and the lowest and most vile, to some people. She did not share that sentiment. Sure, some of them were creatures who once preyed on humans, but she knew that many of them were just misunderstood, and trying to survive in a world that had never been kind to them.

Her articles had cost her so many of her relationships—her parents had stopped speaking to her, many of her friends had shut her out of their lives, and now it seemed like every guy she dated these days couldn't understand her views—either they simply didn't care, or were supporters of President Duli. *There are other things to worry about, you know, Amaya. Stop being so angry. Stop complaining. Why don't you be President instead, if you know so much?*

Was it really possible that her date now was finally...what she wanted?

She went outside and checked her reflection in the mirror. She pulled her hair out of its ponytail, letting it fall down her shoulder in waves. She decided to leave it down. She searched through her bag and swiped on red lipstick over the nude pink shade she had put that morning.

She returned to her seat just as Glen was setting down their orders on the table.

"Are you okay?" Marco asked. "You were gone for some time, I wondered—"

"I'm fine," she assured him. "So. This watermelon sinigang looks *delicious*. Shall we dig in?"

And the rest of their meal passed by in what was perhaps one of the best conversations she had in months—maybe her entire life, even. He was funny, smart, and best of all, sympathetic to her cause. From her writing they moved on to their interests, which they also had a number in common. They didn't exactly agree on everything, and they had a few friendly debates during the conversation, but they agreed on the important things—at least, the things important to her.

It was perfect.

"Okay, okay, I'll have to agree with you that Aisha De Guzman *is* very good," she said as she sipped the last spoonful of the soup of her sinigang, wishing she could have more, just as she wished she had more than an hour of lunch with this man. "And her movies are feel-good and inspiring, which Bathala knows we need more of right now. Her new movie is coming out this week, right?"

"Ah, yes. 'Bukang Liwayway', right?"

"Yeah," she said. "Maybe you'd like to see it sometime?" She suddenly looked down at her plate. This was a first, actually being the one to ask for a second date.

He didn't say anything. She bit her lip, wondering if she had said too much.

"Yes. I…I would like that."

She looked up at him at that, a little puzzled. He was looking out the window now, the distant look in his eyes back again. And the way he said it, too, so wistfully. Like…

Like it was something he wanted, but couldn't have.

Glen appeared before them again, timing impeccable, as always. "Would you like dessert, ma'am, sir?" he asked as he cleared their plates. "Or coffee?"

Amaya glanced at her watch. "Oh, it's 12:30," she said. "You have that client meeting at 1, right? And I do have to get back to the office." To Glen, she said, "We'll have the check, please."

"Wait, you work in The Archipelago Times, right?" Marco said. "That's along the way to where I'm meeting my client. We're meeting in Pasong Tirad. I can drop you off, if you want."

Oh, Bathala. Alone with this perfect man for a few more minutes in his car? She whispered a silent prayer to the heavens, and said, "You sure that's not too much trouble? Thanks, that's really kind of you."

Their check arrived, and Marco of course volunteered to pay. He was about to get his wallet, when he froze.

"You're not Glen," he said to the waiter.

"Sorry, sir," the waiter said. "Glen's occupied right now, and he asked me to give you the check."

Amaya looked at Marco again in bewilderment, because a glint had appeared in his eyes when the waiter said that. But he didn't say anything more, and only laid bills on the tray, which the waiter received with thanks. "Keep the change," he called out to the waiter.

Amaya's eyebrows furrowed. "What was that about—"

Marco suddenly stepped towards her, and she took a step back in surprise. His face moved towards hers, and all she could think of was, wait, is he going to kiss me now, what—

But he only leaned over to whisper in her ear, "You're in danger. I'm going to grab your hand, so hold on to me, okay? We're going to make a run for it."

"What—"

"Trust me, Amaya."

And he *did* grab her hand then, and he began to run, dragging her along.

"Wait…what the hell is… Wait—"

They burst out of the restaurant. They pushed through the usual bustling crowd of the mall complex where the restaurant was located. His hand firmly gripped Amaya's arm, and it was all she could do to not stumble on the path as she followed along. He ran towards the stairs that led down to the mall's basement parking.

"We just need to get to my car," he huffed as they ran down the stairs, "and I'll explain more in detail there. But they're after you."

"What? Who the hell is after me?"

"Duli sent them."

Her eyes widened, she felt like they were going to bulge out of her sockets. "But why—"

"Your last article exposing the deaths of the Lamang Lupa in Digos," he said. "They would have just let that go, but people were beginning to listen to you." He smiled, but mirthlessly. "And Duli doesn't want people doubting him, no."

"Wait, so this whole thing was just a—"

"Oh, no."

He suddenly stopped at the bottom of

the stairs. She was about to collide into him, but he caught her in time. For a moment her face was buried in his chest, and his scent filled her senses. He pulled away and glared at the door.

"Um, why aren't we going out?" she asked.

He pointed at the sign above the door, which said 'Basement Level 1'. "We've run two flights of stairs already, and yet we're still on the same level."

"We're running around in circles?" she gasped. "But how—"

"I was afraid of this," he said. He suddenly took off his shirt.

"What the—" Amaya's jaw slackened. She stood there, frozen, staring at his suddenly half-naked form, her eyes tracing the crests and valleys of his chest and abs.

She suddenly had an image of running her hand through them, committing every inch of his skin to her memory—

"Take off your clothes, Amaya," he said.

Damn, that voice just seemed to slide off her skin, like smooth velvet—

With a great effort of will, she closed her eyes, letting out a little pained cry just as he was beginning to take off his pants.

"Amaya!" he said. He put his hands on her shoulders and shook her slightly. "I'm sorry, but you have to hurry. Take off your clothes now. They probably have a tikbalang with them, or forcing one to use his magic on us, that's why we keep going back to the same door. The only way to counteract a tikbalang's magic is to take off your clothes, then wear them again inside out."

"Oh." She took her hands away from her eyes and quickly turned around so she wouldn't see his naked form. "Oh…"

His tone was apologetic. "I promise I won't look. But please hurry." There was a pounding above them. "I locked the door behind me, but it won't take long for them to get it open."

Thank God she was wearing a one-piece dress, so it didn't take long for her to take her clothes off and wear them inside out. When she was done she turned around, and saw him facing away from her, his hands over his eyes. She pulled his hands away. "I'm ready," she said, sliding her hand into his.

They ran down again. There was a crash above them, and then footsteps, getting closer and closer.

They finally reached the door, and they ran out towards the parking lot. He stopped before a grey SUV and jumped inside, and she tumbled into the passenger seat. They tore out of the parking lot and into the street outside.

He glanced behind them. "This wasn't supposed to happen. They're better at tracking than we thought—"

"Wait," Amaya cut in. "Wait. You promised to explain. So explain."

"Duli's men had been watching you for months," he said. "They first wanted to discredit you, but your record was spotless—there was nothing they could charge you with, unlike with that other reporter, Teresa Sta. Maria? And then you published that article. So they decided you were going to have an 'accident' instead."

"An accident?"

"With your supposed date," he said. "They created this Marco person on the app for you. You were going to meet him, and he was going to lead you somewhere, and you would...get into that accident."

She gasped, both hands covering her mouth.

"They did it before to the reporters in Digos," he said. "Jimmy Magdiwang. Eileen Dimaculangan. That's why you couldn't get hold of them to interview for your article. Jimmy was killed in a supposed police raid, while Eileen just...disappeared."

"He...he wouldn't," she said. "He wouldn't dare to be so bold."

"It's been done before, hasn't it?" he

said. "By the other Diwata dictator he admires so much. Which people have forgotten. Those were peaceful times, they now say." He snorted. "The kind of peace that comes with death."

"So…" Her head still refused to wrap around the truth. "So you're not Marco."

"No," he said. "I intercepted his account, and pretended to be him, so I can meet you somewhere else, and earlier than you were supposed to meet him, to buy us time. I was supposed to take you to the safe house after, where you can hide for the time being. At least until we figure out what to do to ensure your safety from here on. Glen was supposed to be our lookout." He let out a breath. "I hope he's okay."

"You keep saying 'we'." She bit her lip. "Who are they? Are you part of the

Organisation?"

He raised an eyebrow. "No. We're not rebels. But we *are* an organisation, of sorts. We don't want another Saguday to rule this land, that's all. And we don't want anyone getting hurt. Especially not you, Amaya."

And the way he said the last sentence—so earnest and sincere—made her heart twist that she almost forgave him for his deception. Almost.

"You were going to kidnap me," she said.

"What?"

"That's what you were going to do, weren't you?" she said. "You were going to say you were going to take me to my office, but you were going to take me to the safe house instead. That's still kidnapping. And lying. How does that make you different from them? Why the hell should I trust you?"

"That's not what I—" His expression turned rueful. "Wait. You're right. But I would have explained the whole thing to you on the way, and I promise you *can* trust us—"

"Couldn't you have told me the truth somehow through some other way? And I don't know, a lot *earlier*? Instead of letting me believe that it was *finally* a good date, probably the best I've ever had, when all along it was just a lie that I—"

A black car suddenly barrelled into the road from the sidewalk on their right, and Marco swerved to avoid it, sending them spinning out of control into the other lane. He managed to avoid oncoming traffic, but they hurtled toward the sidewalk, hitting a signpost. The impact jolted Amaya out of her seat, and she hit her head on the dashboard.

Cradling her head, she dimly saw a motorcycle pull up in front of them, occupied by two people riding in tandem. The back rider pulled out something from his pocket, which he pointed straight at Amaya.

It was a gun.

She willed herself to move. She scrambled for the necklace she kept hidden inside her clothes and gripped it in her hand. She held it in front of her face and braced herself for the shot.

But it never came. Suddenly the man gave a sharp cry, and he dropped the gun. The man riding in front looked at him, but he too, suddenly cried out in agony.

Marco got out of the car, that hard glint back in his eyes, his arms stretched out towards the two men, fingers curled into claws. She turned back to the two men, who were both writhing in agony now. The two men opened their mouths to scream, and out of their mouths flew out wasps—hundreds of them. She felt the lunch she had just eaten suddenly lurch out of her stomach and into her throat, and she clamped her hand on her mouth to keep from heaving.

Out of the corner of her eye, she saw a movement. It was another motorcycle pulling up behind Marco, this time occupied only by a single rider.

The man did not bring out a gun. Instead he brought out a knife—long and slender, with a curved blade that glinted silver-blue in the light of the sun. With a cry, Amaya ran out of the car.

The man said a single word and threw the knife straight at Marco's neck.

Amaya threw herself in the path of the knife.

The knife stopped inches before the necklace pendant she kept firmly in front of her face and dropped straight down to the ground with a loud clatter, like an invisible force had stopped it in its tracks. Marco finally realised what was happening and whirled, turning his gaze on the third attacker.

"Get him," he muttered, and the man suddenly screamed as the horde of wasps that had just come out of the two men descended upon him, stinging every part of his skin and crawling into his mouth to devour him from the inside.

Amaya turned away and collided into Marco again, but he wrapped strong arms around her.

When the man's screams finally died down, Marco gently pulled away from her. "The police will be arriving soon. We have to go, Amaya."

She nodded, and without saying another word, they climbed into the car. They drove in complete silence after that. Amaya still clutched her necklace, her hands still shaking.

"Is that necklace an anting-anting?" Marco said, finally breaking the silence. "It created a shield."

"Yes," Amaya said. "A gift from a former History professor."

"You saved my life back there. Thank

you."

She couldn't look at him. "You're…you're a Mambabarang."

A pause. And then, "Yes."

"When did you put the wasp eggs in their bodies?"

"When they were chasing after us in the mall stairwell."

"So the fully grown wasps burst out of them at the right time." She swallowed. "You're…you're a Lamang Lupa."

She had been defending them for most of her life, but this was the first time she had ever seen a Lamang Lupa in action. And…actually killing.

It was terrifying.

"Yes." His gaze hardened. "You thought I was a Diwata, didn't you?" When she didn't reply, he continued, a little bitterly, "Well, I'm sorry to disappoint you. I am a Lamang Lupa, a monster, borne out of darkness, with powers so terrifying, we can't possibly be anything but evil. We do not deserve to live, like Duli says. Maybe you regret defending us now, now that you see what we can do to people."

"I'm sorry," she said, finally looking at him. "I do admit that I *did* wonder if you were a Diwata. And I really *was* scared when I saw how you killed those three men. But…"

She took a deep breath before going on. "You did save me. And now helping me to escape. And I think…I think it's not really what your power is that determines if you're good or evil. I mean, Diwata like Duli can kill, too, right? It's what you choose to do with those powers that determine that."

He didn't say anything in reply to that, but she saw that his eyes had softened.

They were silent for several minutes after that, as they cruised along the highway. It wasn't until they stopped in front of a small nipa hut in the middle of a rice field did he speak again.

"We're here," he said. "This place is protected by strong magic, so you'll be safe here." He glanced at her. "If you have decided to trust us, that is."

"Yeah, I guess," she said. "Even though you did lie to me." She sighed. "I was just disappointed that it wasn't a real date after all."

He leaned towards her and looked straight into her eyes. "It wasn't completely a lie. I meant everything else I said when we were on that date."

His face broke into a small smile. "I really had a great time with you, Amaya."

He got out of the car, and Amaya followed him again. He waved to the woman who had stepped out from the hut and introduced Amaya to her. The woman looked like she was in her thirties and was ordinarily dressed in a white t-shirt and jeans, but she was very beautiful. He called her Lady Makiling. Amaya glanced up at the dormant volcano silhouetted in the distance behind the woman, which was also called by the same name. She wondered if the woman really was as ordinary as she seemed.

"Lady Makiling will take care of you in the meantime," he said. "We'll find a way so you can get back to the city, eventually. Goodbye, Amaya.”

“I think you hit your head,” Lady Makiling said. “Let me take a look, let’s go inside.”

Amaya was about to follow the woman, but stopped. “Excuse me, Lady Makiling, I’ll be back.”

She ran after Marco.

“Wait,” she said. He stopped and looked quizzically at her. “Marco’s not your real name, isn’t it?”

He looked surprised at that. “No.”

“What is it, then?”

His lips eased into a smile. “My real name is Solaiman.”

“Solaiman,” she said. “Well, that suits you better than Marco, I guess.” She held out her hand, and he took it. “Nice to meet you, Solaiman. See you next week.”

"Next week?" he said, raising an eyebrow.

"I told you 'Bukang Liwayway' is coming out next week, right?" She glanced at the hut behind them. "Cell reception is probably terrible here, and Lady Makiling doesn't look like the type of person who uses the internet, so you can at least download that movie somewhere and bring a copy for me to watch here." She moved closer towards him. "I mean, it's going to get boring out here. And…lonely." She bit her lower lip as she smiled at him. "You can do that for me, right?"

He put a finger beneath her chin and tilted her face up towards his.

"I can do that," he said, his voice husky as ever. He leaned over closer to her. "And more, if you want," he whispered, breath warm on her earlobe.

She shivered a little as she leaned into him.

He pulled away with a grin. "See you next week then, Amaya."

She watched him leave, still with a smile on her face.

Well, she was right, that everything *was* too good to be true, and nothing was really as it seemed. And yet, as far as first dates went, it was pretty great. More than that, actually.

It was perfect.

Ode to Cleo and Ant
By D.J. Elton

Once such a fine pair.

Every morning at 1am, Ant comes and gently taps Cleo's shoulder. She sighs loudly. He tenderly strokes her weary sleeping face, then he sees her long black wig on top of the dressing table near her head. An ugly sign of mortality, he thinks, and involuntarily shudders.

The queen appears to gasp and snore loudly. Her chin wobbles and a trail of silvery saliva sticks along her cheek. Ant surveys the bedroom. Two empty bottles of black market brew poke out from under the messy bed.

Cleo is a large woman. Now her clothes are strewn like sad sheets over the nearest chairs and tables. *She has not aged gracefully*, thinks Ant sadly as he distastefully sniffs the dank air.

He thinks about the nymphs and sirens, the beauty of young flesh. After all, it's only history, and he has been so blessed to stay in the physical plane for so much longer.

The Long-Distance Relationship

By Galina Trefil

With fresh flowers, he visited her grave each month. When he departed, she wandered the cemetery, lonely and counting down the days until he returned. As much as she missed him, it didn't occur to her to complain. Seeing other graves entirely ignored, she was grateful for his continued devotion.

Then suddenly, he stopped coming. She didn't understand. What had happened to him? Had he forgotten her? Was he hurt? Surely, he couldn't be dead, or they would finally be together again!

At least, they would have been if only their families hadn't opted to bury them in separate cemeteries.

The Stranger in the Waiting Room
By Meera Dandekar

It was an unspoken rule to never ask anyone what they're in here for. She broke the rule.

The receptionist's call had echoed in the living room when I automated message said, "Your session has been rescheduled. Please check in fifteen minutes to confirm your session. Thank you." Something was wrong. Dr Felix never rescheduled any of his sessions.

I argued with myself—go now or just cancel. Dr Felix had been suggested to me by numerous people, and if he was the one to help me fix myself, I needed to be there. I don't know if it was fate or something else, but my gut told me to be there. I made it in time, in fact, with three minutes to spare.

"I'm sorry, but your session will start in an hour. You may take a seat and we'll be right with you." I wasn't sure if they were kidding or if this was serious, but I took a seat anyway. I didn't have much to do at home. I picked up a magazine from the stack that was neatly arranged on the coffee table. It was a shame that there was not one manly magazine here. I pulled out my phone and scrolled through the news section. Nothing interesting caught my attention, so I shifted to a different platform.

I was watching the fifth video on how to make cupcakes with just four ingredients when the door opened. The sun seemed to push her inside the waiting room, and she glided inside, letting the door close behind her. She did not even glance at me. She walked straight to the reception desk. I tried to not pay attention to her and pretended to be deeply interested in the rigorous beating of the eggs. I couldn't help but overhear the conversation. Her hair was left untouched, falling over her shoulder, hugging her waist.

"Excuse me, I have an appointment with Dr Felix at 4 o'clock."

"I'm sorry, your session has been shifted to 5 o'clock. You may take a seat if you wish." I almost heard her curse under her breath. I could see that she wanted to argue about it. She didn't. She walked to the opposite side of the room and took a seat. She picked up Vogue and flipped through it as she sat on the teal couch, one leg crossed over the other. I tried to keep my eyes on the phone screen, but I couldn't help but glance up once in a while.

She must have noticed me staring at her, because she kept glancing at me from time to time.

"Do you want something from me?" She was in a bad mood; I could tell.

"No. I just couldn't help but notice the pen smudge on your face. I'm sorry if I made you uncomfortable." I quickly looked at my phone, avoiding her glare. She got her compact out of her purse to examine the mark and walked to the bathroom. I tried not to watch her go. I shouldn't be staring at a random woman, especially here. She came back with even more makeup than she had on before. Who was she even trying to impress? Her therapist! She caught me staring at her again, and I kept my gaze on the floor.

"So what are you in here for?" she asked. Both the receptionist and I looked at her.

"I thought we weren't supposed to ask that to the other patients here." I raised my eyebrow at her, causing her to roll her eyes.

"It's not like I'm going to go around telling everyone. If you're here and I'm here, I guess we're both going through some problems we don't want to face alone." She leaned back before continuing. "Not that I'm forcing you to answer." She turned her head away from me. I started to feel that she was difficult to keep up with.

"I've been through a traumatic situation recently. I was suggested to come here by my doctor. Dr Felix seems to have laid his ground. I've not heard another psychiatrist's name when they all tried to suggest one to me." She wanted me to go on, but I could see the receptionist's keen eyes on me, and I felt uncomfortable.

"That's awful. I'm sorry." She smiled at me. I wasn't sure if I was crossing the boundary, but I asked her the same question.

"They say I have bipolar disorder. My boyfriend, well, my ex-boyfriend thought I was crazy. He had signed us up for couple's therapy. That's where they said that I might have some other issues. They sent him out of the room to have a private conversation. By the time I was done, he was already gone. If I ever see him again, he won't be able to walk or have children." She had made this more awkward than it was. I wasn't sure how I was supposed to react to this, so I kept my mouth shut. I just gave her a slight nod and pretended to be engrossed in my phone.

"This is your first session, right?"

"That's right." I didn't look up, but she didn't take the hint. She continued talking.

"He is really great. You'd definitely

like him." I just agreed with her and walked to the bathroom.

I splashed some water on my face and checked the time. Only twenty minutes had passed since I had come in. I was hoping it would be an hour. I was dreading going back out.

From the waiting room, I could hear her voice, talking to someone else. It was probably the receptionist—she was the only one there. Then I heard the door beside the men's bathroom close. I walked out to see her sitting there, flipping through a different magazine. The receptionist was gone.

When she saw me approach, she shifted slightly on the couch to invite me. She smiled as I took my place beside her.

"I'm Anna." She offered her hand, and

I shook it.

John. So you are scheduled for five. I'm probably scheduled just after you," I said, trying to make conversation.

"They haven't told you the time yet?"

I shook my head. "There was a mix up."

"The same thing happened to me. I was actually scheduled for 4 o'clock, but I received a call saying that I had to come right that moment or it would be scheduled to next week. So I rushed here, almost forgetting my purse in the process." She patted her bag to indicate that she hadn't forgotten it after all. "When I came here, they told me it's at five. I'm really upset about this because I had to go to the gym too. I might have to cancel. My trainer is going to be annoyed that I've missed another day."

I didn't want her to know that I had already overheard everything.

"You can tell them that you were occupied here," I suggested.

"No way! I'm not telling anyone that I see a therapist." She turned slightly, and I felt that it was an indication to keep my distance.

We didn't speak for a couple of moments.

"I'm sorry if I'm being pushy or rude," she said.

I was shocked at this statement. I didn't expect her to cave like that.

"You aren't. It's boring to just sit here. It's nice to have someone to talk to." This seemed to bring the colour back to her face. I wasn't sure if I should tell her anything about it. I hadn't even told Dr Felix yet.

My phone started to play the video from where I had left off, aloud. I quickly scrambled to shut it off, but instead, I dropped it. Anna picked it up and flipped the phone to check for cracks. She almost chuckled.

"It came in recommendations," I said.

"I'm not judging you. I have no place to. Also, they don't work. I can give you a better recipe if you want to bake some cupcakes." She was looking down at my phone.

"That would be great," I said, smiling.

She took a breath. I was guessing that she wanted to ask me something but decided against it. I looked at her longer than I should have. She looked like someone who would make you comfortable. Even if she was straightforward, she seemed like a warm-hearted person.

"I don't know if you want to talk about it, but are you okay?" She seemed genuinely concerned. She would be the first person I would tell if I decided to ever talk about it. She was a stranger. It was probably better. I might not even meet her after this. How is it easier to pour your heart out to a complete stranger than someone you know?

"My brother and I got into an accident last month. He didn't make it. We wanted to take a break from life so we had decided to take a road trip, for old time's sake. We drank a lot while driving because the roads were empty at night. We were still careful. The truck came at us from nowhere. We were careful." Anna didn't say anything. She put her hand on my shoulder in an attempt to comfort me. I put my hand on hers.

"I'm sorry," she said.

I nodded at her apology. I didn't want people to feel sorry for me. I wanted comfort.

"After our sessions are over, I'll buy you some cake. It's better than those cupcakes."

It made me smile.

I could feel a cool breeze blow. I couldn't find the source, but I felt it encircle me. The sunshine inside the room seemed too bright, and yet it was cold. I resisted the urge to look around. I felt something grab my hand, something warm. All of a sudden, it was gone. Everything was back to normal.

The receptionist called for Anna. Dr Felix was ready for her now. As she got up to leave, she placed a hand on my lap. "Everything will be okay." Then she left. I checked my watch and forty minutes had passed. I just had to wait another hour before it was my turn to enter that room.

The waiting room felt lonely again. I peeked over the reception desk to see the receptionist was back, making phone calls. I didn't even notice her take her seat. She saw me looking over. She placed the phone back in its place.

"I hope she didn't annoy you. She actually has a condition I can't tell you about. She's a nice person otherwise. She just tends to blurt out sometimes."

I didn't like that she had called Anna

annoying. I didn't find her annoying at all. In fact, I thought she was a good person, a good friend who would hold your hand in dark times. I didn't understand what the receptionist was talking about. I just nodded along and let her get back to work. I picked up the magazine Anna was reading. It was boring, so I settled on looking at the pictures instead. I found a perfume trail on the magazine page, and I fought my instincts to run it on myself. It felt as though time had slowed down. I tapped my leg in a rhythm and then moved on to scrolling down my Instagram feed. It was difficult to pass the time alone.

The door opened, and I saw Anna thank Dr Felix for her session. She grabbed her coat. She was leaving.

The receptionist turned to me and said,

"Dr Felix will be ready for you in ten minutes."

"Actually, is it possible to reschedule?"

"Sure. Is tomorrow fine with you?"

"Definitely." I took Anna's hand to let her know to wait for me. We left the waiting room, deep in conversation.

I looked back at the empty couch, and for a split second, I thought I saw my brother. Anna looked back and then at me. I just smiled and led her out.

Storm Inheritance
By Stacey Jaine McIntcosh

The wind toyed with her hair. A storm was coming. She had known her entire life that she was different, but she hadn't expected to find out how different. She was a Demi God. The daughter of Thor.

"Audra!"

She was standing outside in the wind

and the rain. Drawing in power. The kind of power he would never know.

A mortal life was so fleeting. And yet she loved him all the more because of it.

Her command of the element of Air? She'd give it all up, just to exist, captured solely by the love in his eyes.

The Selfie
By Ximena Escobar

They were the glow of wonder, lingering
    like beauty in ancient ruins,
    more beautiful because it's lost.

    Games of hide and seek in the maze,
    the back of her dress disappearing in

the darkest shades of green

in the darkest dark where they loved
each other most.

They were children in a hideaway.

Dear dark wardrobe in the beginning
of memory.

A forest in the depth of their soul,

hugging knees, side by side,

absorbed in the distant sight of stars,

the open sky between the high
branches.

Had it been 100 years?

They sat on the fountain. His arm
wasn't long enough that they could see the
statues behind them within the frame of the
phone. But their view was deep as infinite,

and they travelled all the way to that day that became all the days, right there on that stone. The only time she did smell of mandarins.

And they smiled their underwhelming smiles—they weren't as attractive as they once were. But both inbreathed the cosmic story overfilling their lungs, and fresh laughter sprang like funny fountain drizzle—youthful cheeks rising, sweet dimples sinking.

The hole in the gut sinking.

The gap between the trees opening.

And waves of red hair cascading down her shoulders like a winding path to the dark corners of desire.

They turned a corner in the maze,
They got lost in the darkness.

His tongue circled inside her like a
spiral chasing the centre,
the elusive definition of their love.

There was only a mandarin tree,
its everlasting fruits of everlasting
rum,
everlasting swelling
of throats and verses,
featuring oranges and Italian palaces.
They were so drunk in love, but so out
of love too,
because flesh is the bond
that bears
the dullness of reality,
and quenches the vertigo.

Little palms unsticking in the starry
sky,

having to go through it all,
alone.

His Rolex said it was 6pm. This time tomorrow they'll be hugging each other goodbye on the platform, possibly for the last time as they each return—he to the ashes, she to the grave. They'll think, as always, of each other next they rise, happy to be where they belong.

Happy to miss each other,
hand in hand with those who became their future,
everything they were so afraid of.
And a new seed planted by their naked bone embrace
blossoming orange in the overspilling fountain

of their memories.

Neither cared for a hangover and both were disappointed that those days were truly over. Yet, they swirled their Aperol Spritzers and it seemed a blink before they found themselves swimming, fully clothed, in the sunrise.

Taking selfies of a delightful shine,
the ineradicable
joy,
of their love.

First published, *Organic Ink* Dragon Soul Press 2019

Falling in Love
By Zoey Xolton

Michael took a deep breath. A hundred lifetimes had passed since he'd killed her, and still his heart ached. He'd only been a new vampire then, not yet in control of the curse—the bloodlust—which afflicted his kind.

It was time. He wouldn't endure another night without her.

He just couldn't.

Throwing wide the castle doors, he met the sun with open arms. His golden hair caught fire, then his flesh blistered and peeled, before his entire form burst into flame.

As his damned soul burned, he saw her ghost—she beckoned to him.

"I forgive you, my love."

ABOUT THE PUBLISHER

BLACK HARE PRESS is a small, independent publisher based in Melbourne, Australia.

Founded in 2018, our aim has always been to champion emerging authors from all around the globe and offer opportunities for them to participate in speculative fiction and horror short story anthologies.

Connect

Website: *www.blackharepress.com*

Twitter: *@BlackHarePress*